TURTLE QUEST

PIERS HARPER

**For
Joseph and
Thomas**

Copyright © 1997 by Piers Harper

All rights reserved. First U.S. edition 1997

Library of Congress Cataloging-in-Publication Data
Harper, Piers.
Turtle quest / by Piers Harper.—1st U.S. ed.
Summary : Two Mayan children find a jade stone and a map, and with t
of a talking pig and some magical bees, they set out to find the tu
mentioned in an ancient legend.
ISBN 1-56402-959-X
1. Mayas—Juvenile fiction. [1. Toy and movable books—Specimen
2. Mayas—Fiction. 3. Indians of Mexico—Fiction. 4. Picture puzz
5. Toy and movable books.] I. Title.
PZ7.H2319Tu 1996 96-16136

2 4 6 8 10 9 7 5 3 1

Printed in Hong Kong

This book was typeset in Kosmik and Stemple Schneidler 2.
The pictures were done in ink.

CANDLEWICK PRESS

2067 MASSACHUSETTS AVENUE
CAMBRIDGE, MASSACHUSETTS 02140

Xoc took the jade stone from the bag, then reached in again and pulled out a map. It showed the lands of their people, the Mayans.

"What is the turtle that is the world?"
they asked the village priest. "And how can we seek it?"

"Only I know the truth about the turtle," interrupted a small plump animal sitting nearby. "My name is Pacal. Listen carefully.

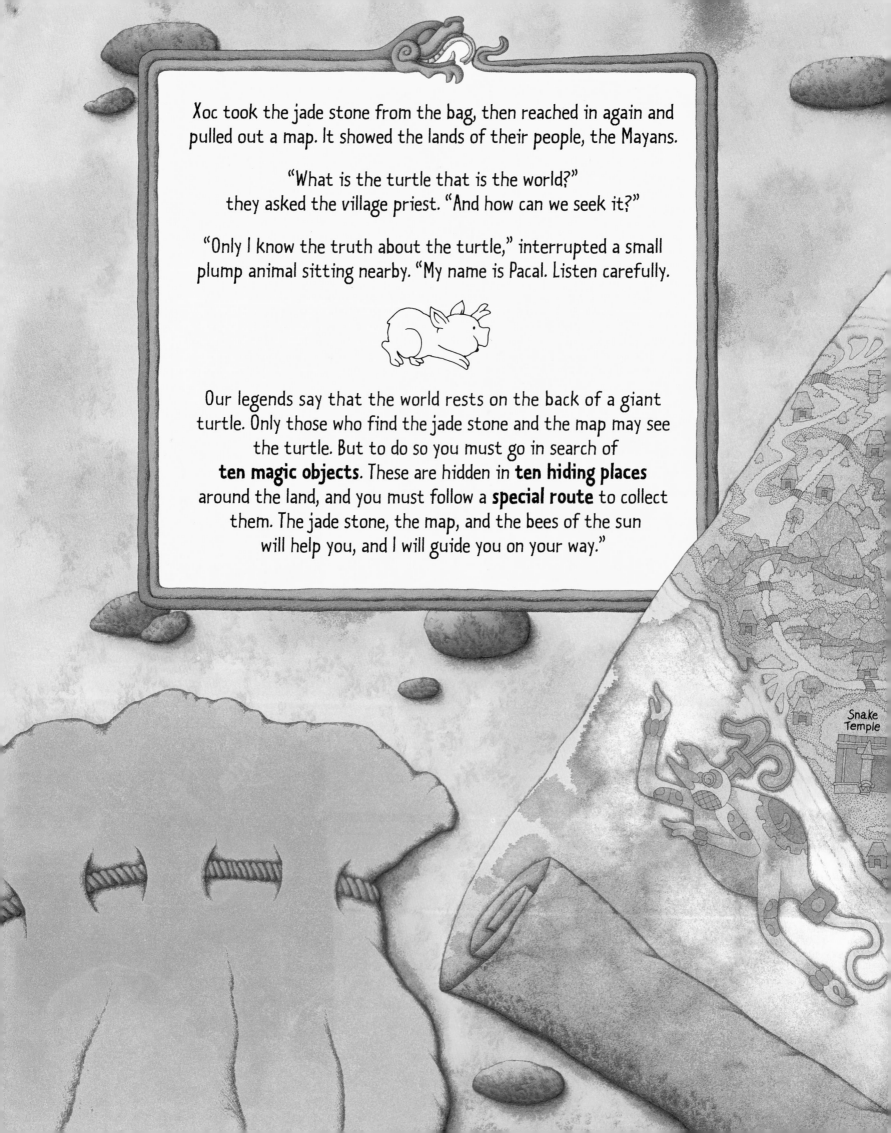

Our legends say that the world rests on the back of a giant turtle. Only those who find the jade stone and the map may see the turtle. But to do so you must go in search of **ten magic objects**. These are hidden in **ten hiding places** around the land, and you must follow a **special route** to collect them. The jade stone, the map, and the bees of the sun will help you, and I will guide you on your way."

Snake
Temple

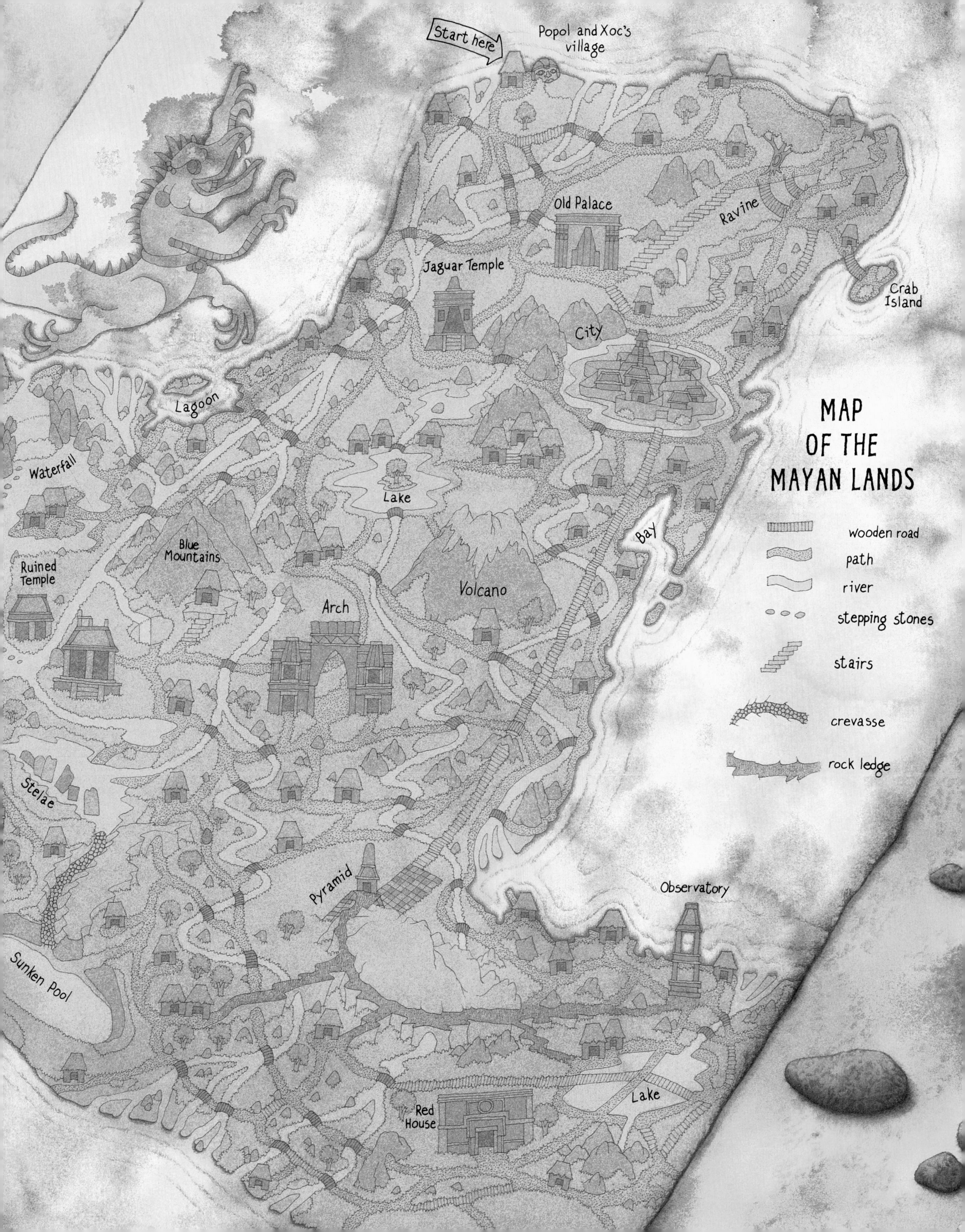
MAP
OF THE
MAYAN LANDS
wooden road
path
river
stepping stones
stairs
crevasse
rock ledge
Start here
Popol and Xoc's village
Old Palace
Ravine
Crab Island
Jaguar Temple
City
Lagoon
Waterfall
Lake
Bay
Blue Mountains
Ruined Temple
Volcano
Arch
Stelae
Pyramid
Observatory
Sunken Pool
Red House
Lake

Reader!

You can help Popol and Xoc, too.

THESE ARE YOUR TASKS

1. Use the jade stone to:

- Find the magic objects
- Discover the hiding places and the special routes
- Overcome dangers and obstacles
- Solve any other problems faced by Popol and Xoc

2. Follow the route on the map of the Mayan lands.

THE QUEST BEGINS HERE IN POPOL AND XOC'S VILLAGE.
This is the first hiding place.

PACAL WILL TELL YOU WHAT TO DO.

ABOUT THE JADE STONE

Take a look at the stone.

 One side has a turtle. Whenever you see this sign you must have this side face up.

 The other side has words and symbols. Whenever you see this sign you must have this side face up.

There are bees in every corner and six windows in the stone.

Now we shall find a magic object.

RED bees always help with this task.

1. Place the jade stone on the picture so that the four corner bees each touch a RED bee.

2. Look through the windows.

Can you see an eye in five of the windows and a symbol in the sixth?

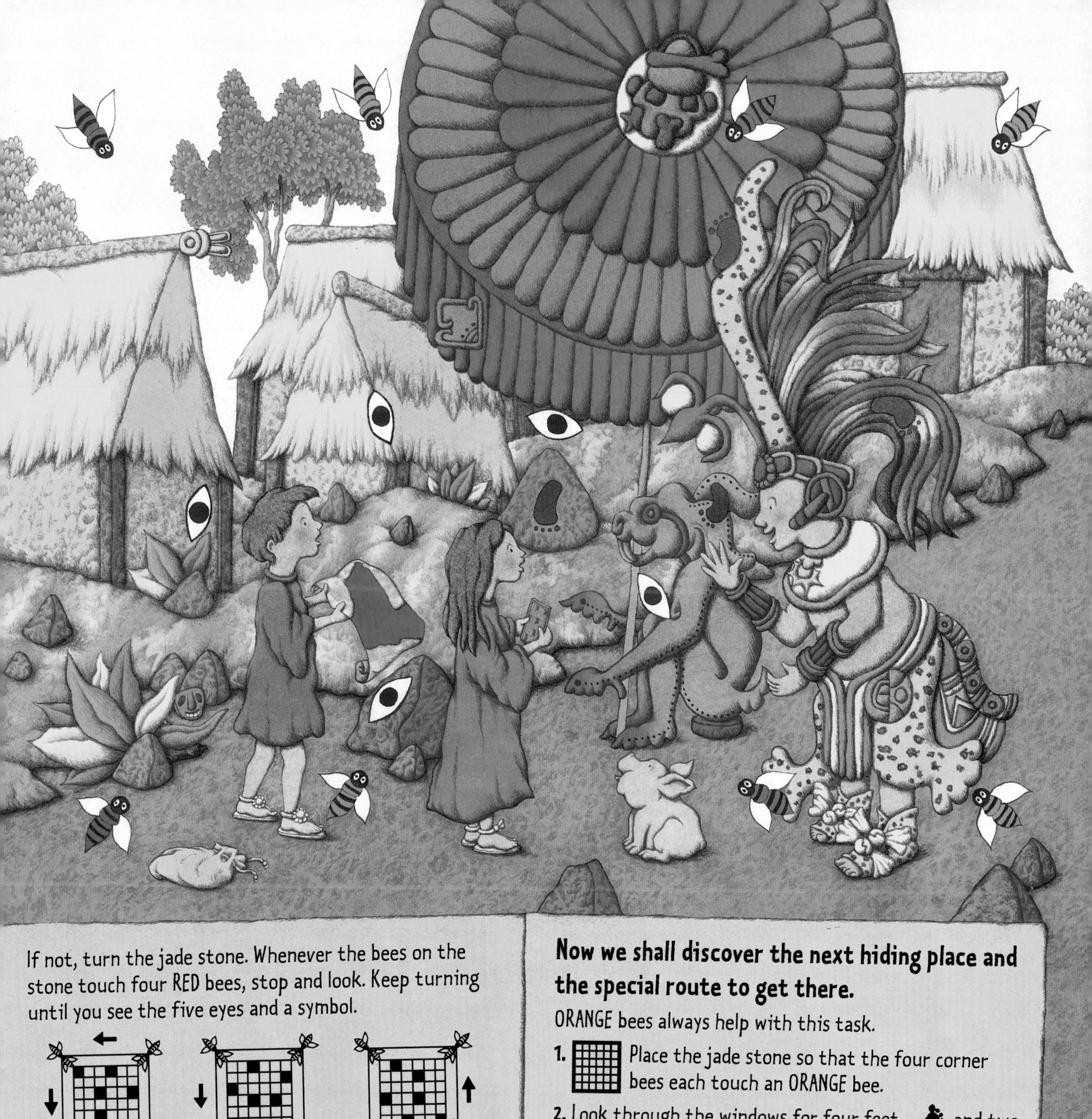

If not, turn the jade stone. Whenever the bees on the stone touch four RED bees, stop and look. Keep turning until you see the five eyes and a symbol.

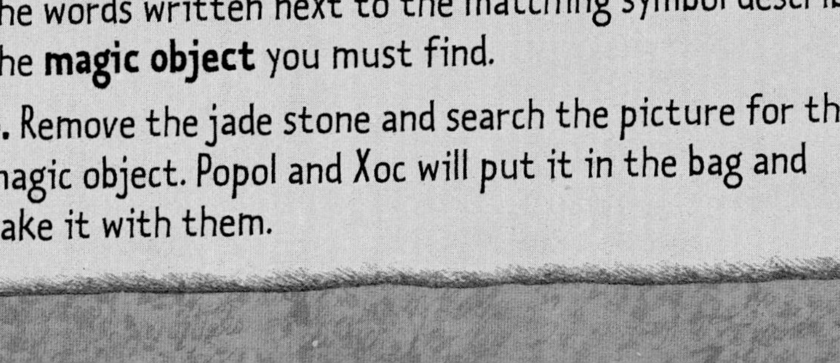

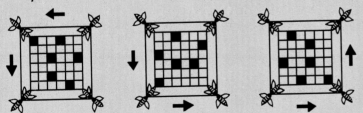

3. Now match the symbol to one on the jade stone. The words written next to the matching symbol describe the **magic object** you must find.

4. Remove the jade stone and search the picture for the magic object. Popol and Xoc will put it in the bag and take it with them.

Now we shall discover the next hiding place and the special route to get there.

ORANGE bees always help with this task.

1. Place the jade stone so that the four corner bees each touch an ORANGE bee.

2. Look through the windows for four feet and two symbols. If you can't find them, turn the jade stone as before, until they appear.

3. Match the symbols to ones on the jade stone. The words next to them tell you the next **hiding place** to visit and the **special route** to get there.

4. Now look at the map to follow your special route to the next hiding place. **Found it? Turn the page. Let's go!**

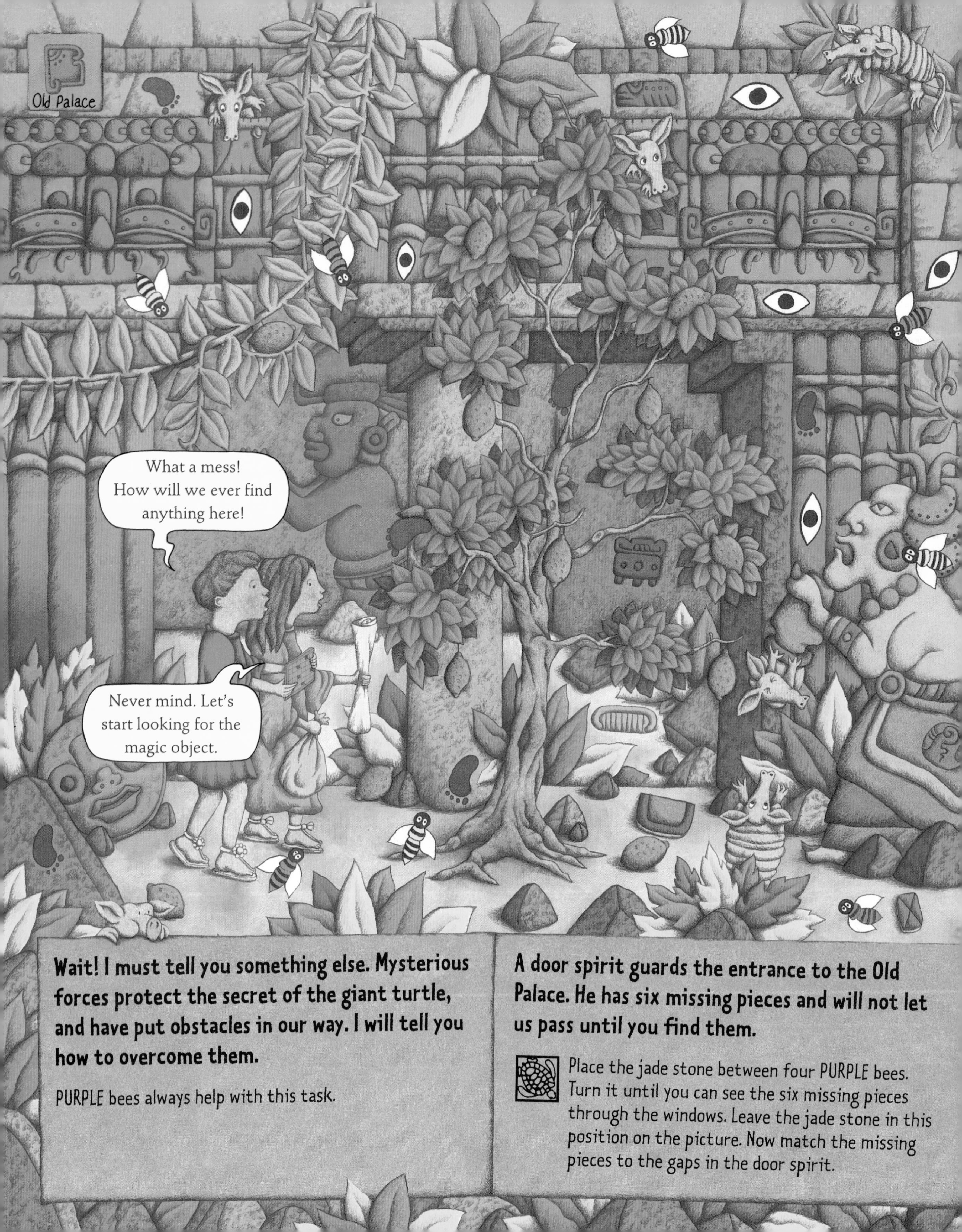
Old Palace
What a mess! How will we ever find anything here!
Never mind. Let's start looking for the magic object.

Wait! I must tell you something else. Mysterious forces protect the secret of the giant turtle, and have put obstacles in our way. I will tell you how to overcome them.

PURPLE bees always help with this task.

A door spirit guards the entrance to the Old Palace. He has six missing pieces and will not let us pass until you find them.

Place the jade stone between four PURPLE bees. Turn it until you can see the six missing pieces through the windows. Leave the jade stone in this position on the picture. Now match the missing pieces to the gaps in the door spirit.

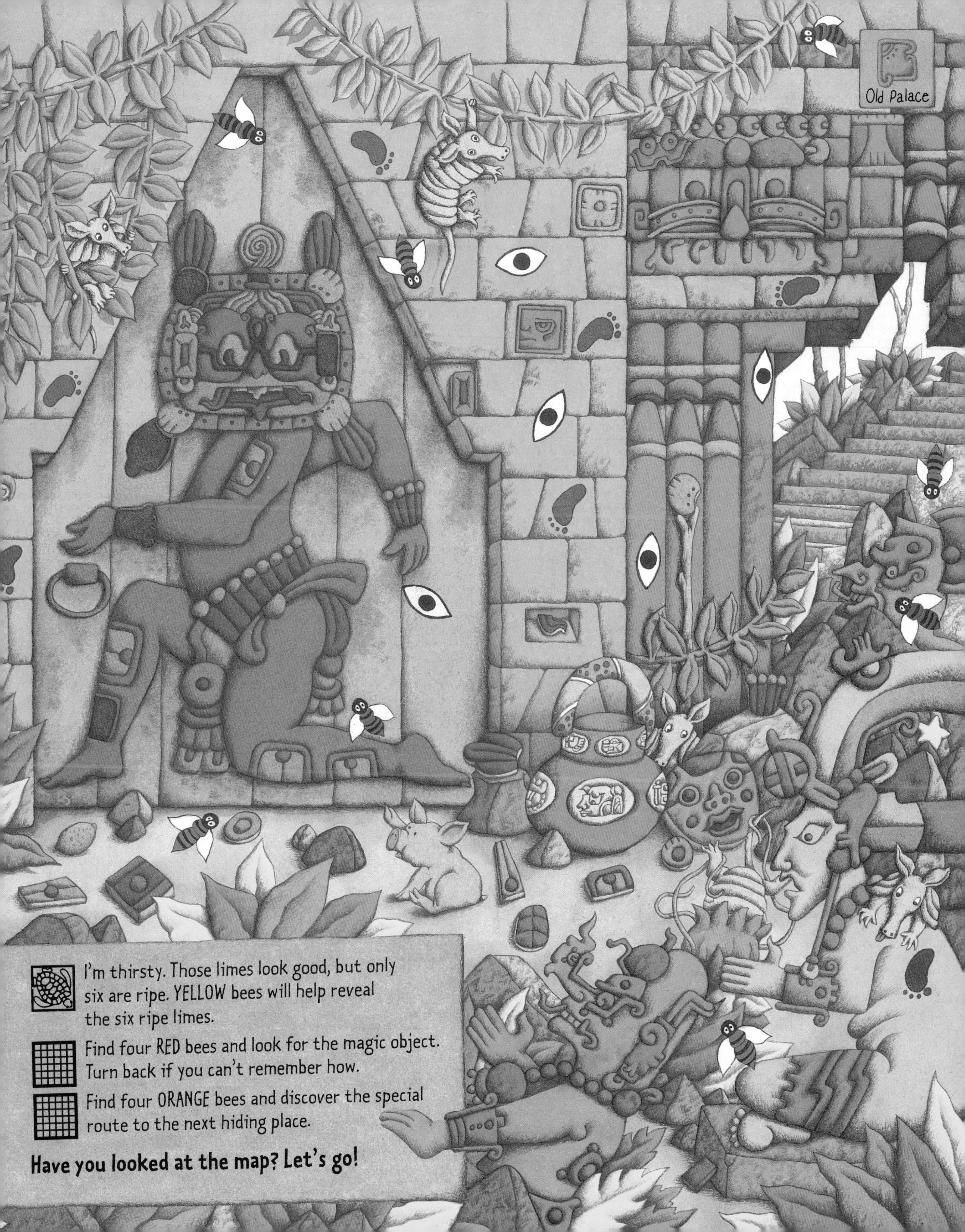
Old Palace

I'm thirsty. Those limes look good, but only six are ripe. YELLOW bees will help reveal the six ripe limes.

Find four RED bees and look for the magic object. Turn back if you can't remember how.

Find four ORANGE bees and discover the special route to the next hiding place.

Have you looked at the map? Let's go!

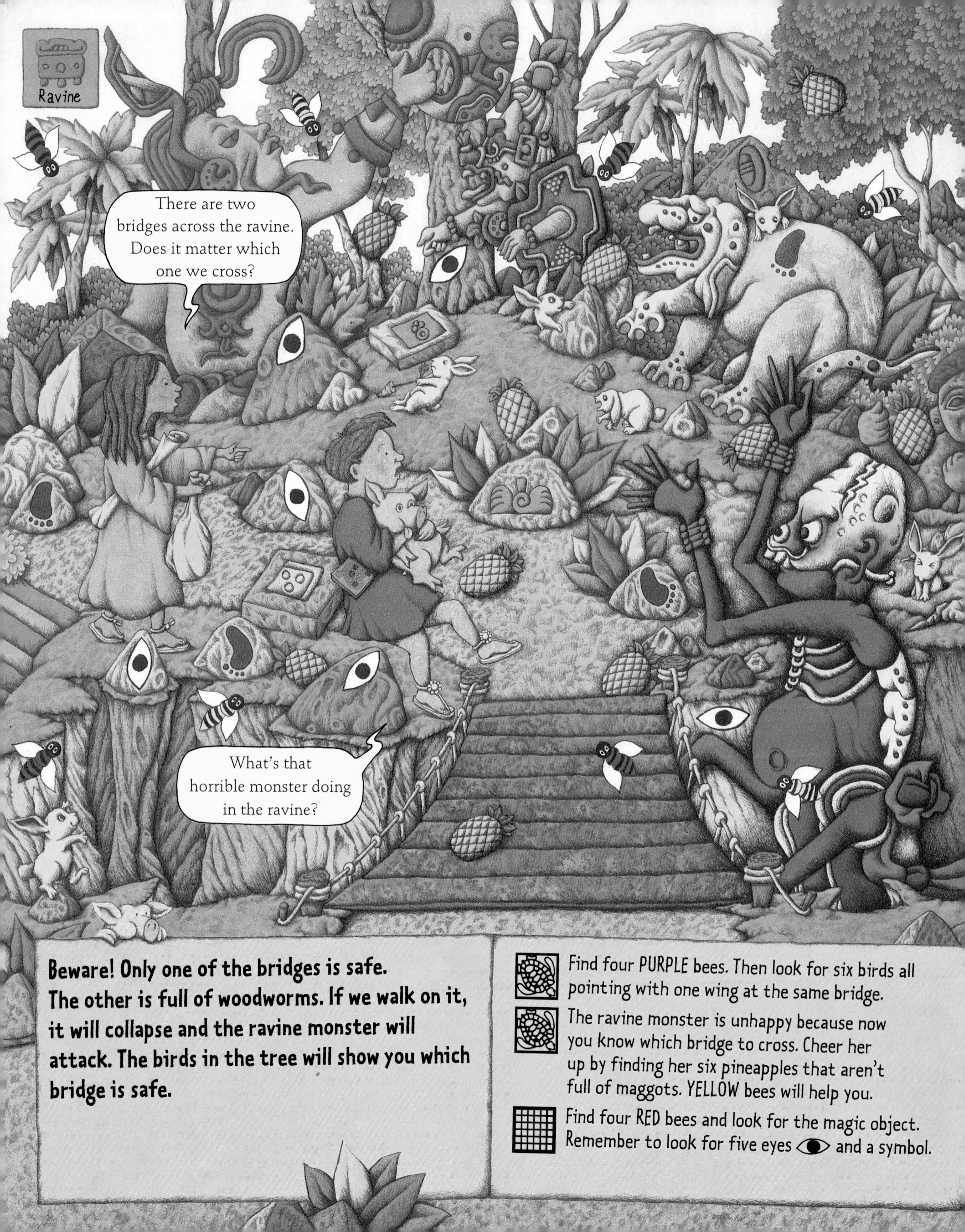
Ravine
There are two bridges across the ravine. Does it matter which one we cross?
What's that horrible monster doing in the ravine?

Beware! Only one of the bridges is safe. The other is full of woodworms. If we walk on it, it will collapse and the ravine monster will attack. The birds in the tree will show you which bridge is safe.

Find four PURPLE bees. Then look for six birds all pointing with one wing at the same bridge.

The ravine monster is unhappy because now you know which bridge to cross. Cheer her up by finding her six pineapples that aren't full of maggots. YELLOW bees will help you.

Find four RED bees and look for the magic object. Remember to look for five eyes and a symbol.

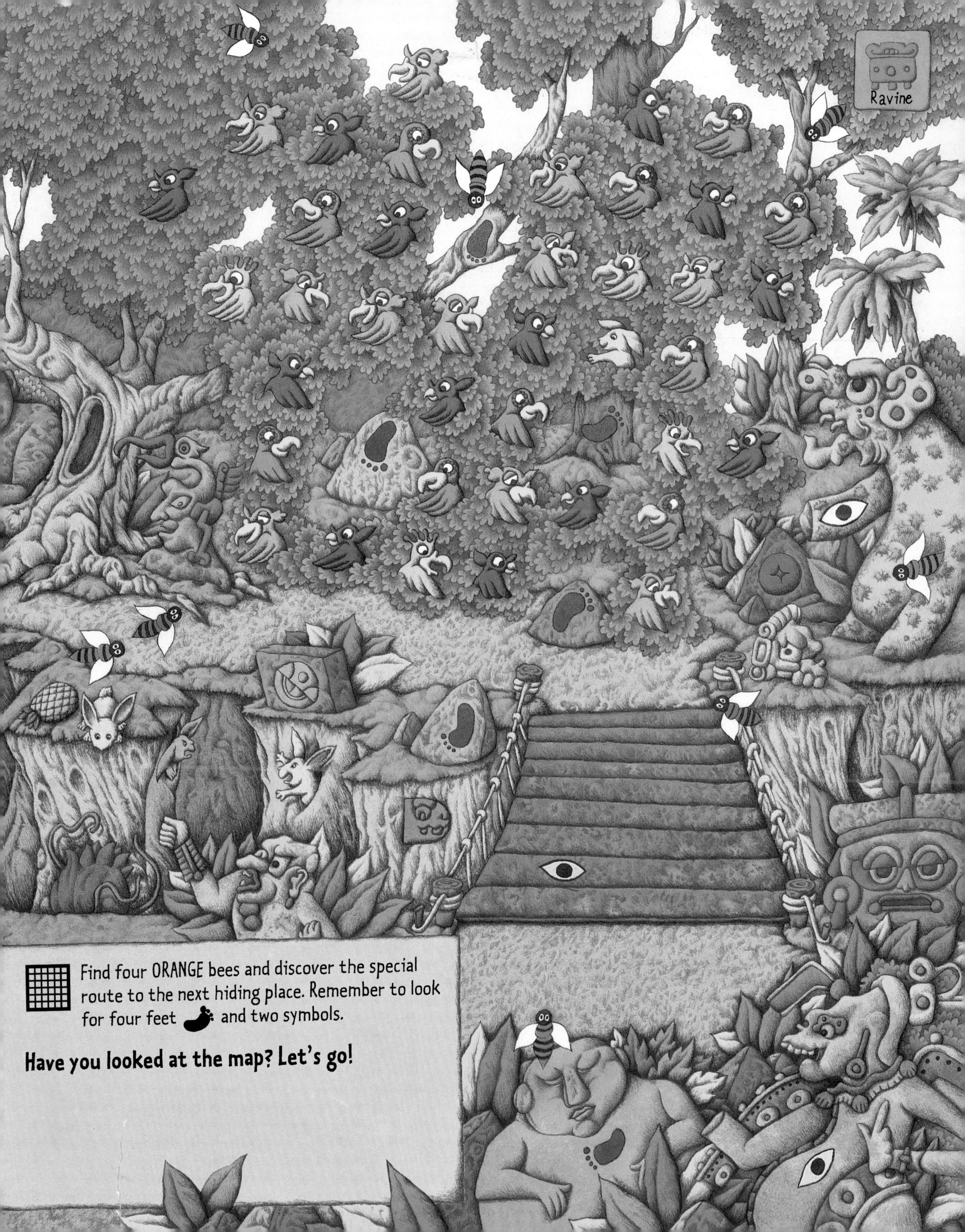
Ravine

Find four ORANGE bees and discover the special route to the next hiding place. Remember to look for four feet and two symbols.

Have you looked at the map? Let's go!

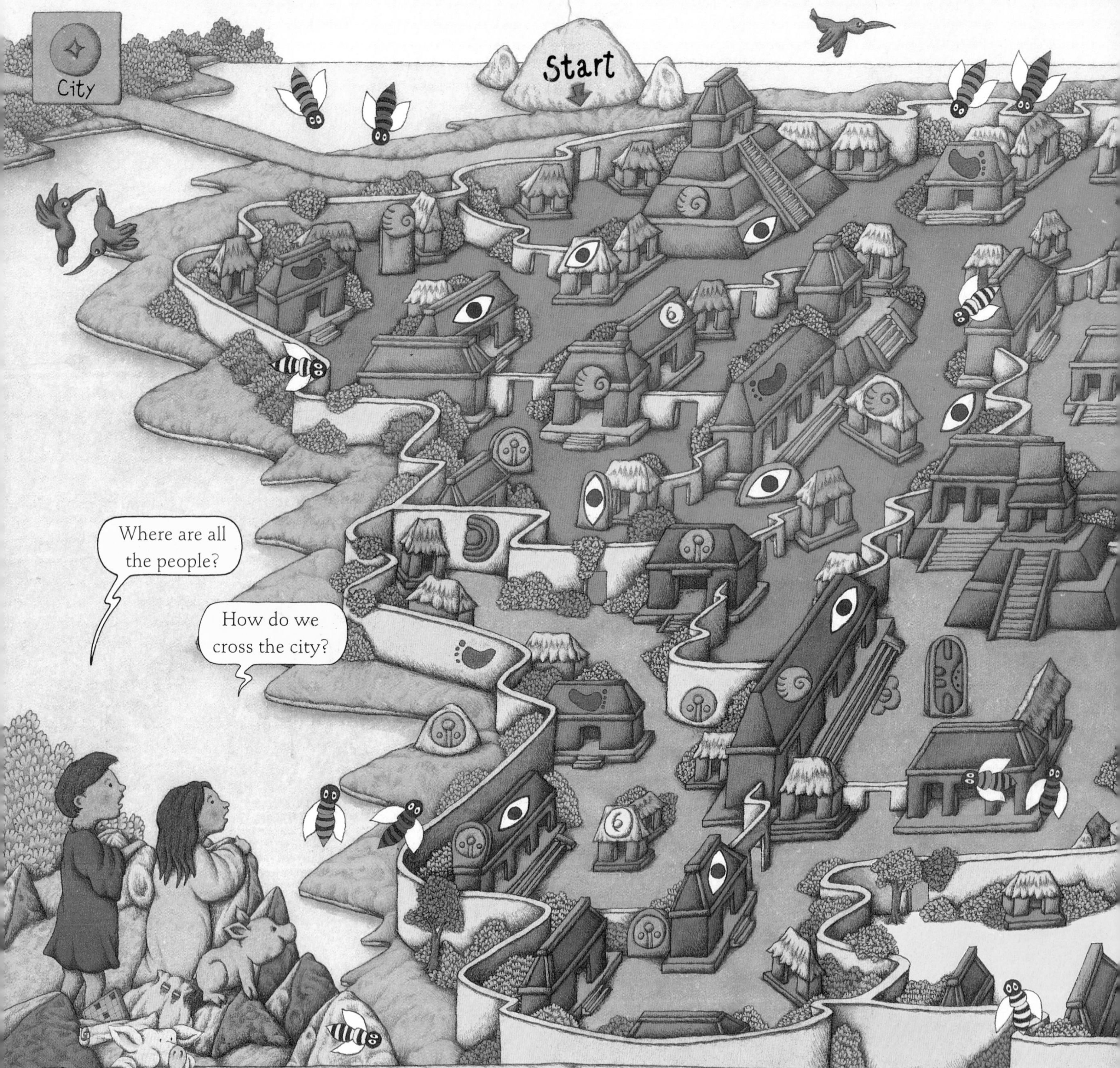
City
Start
Where are all the people?
How do we cross the city?

This city is dangerous! The people are at war with each other. They sleep all day and fight all night! There is one safe route through the city's four zones and we must find it. Hurry!

BLUE, YELLOW, PURPLE, and then PINK bees will help with this task. Find four BLUE bees. When you can see identical symbols in five of the windows, the sixth window will reveal a door. Remove the jade stone and find the shortest way through the red zone from the door labeled "Start" to this door. Travel from door to door through the other zones in the same way. The final door leads you out of the city.

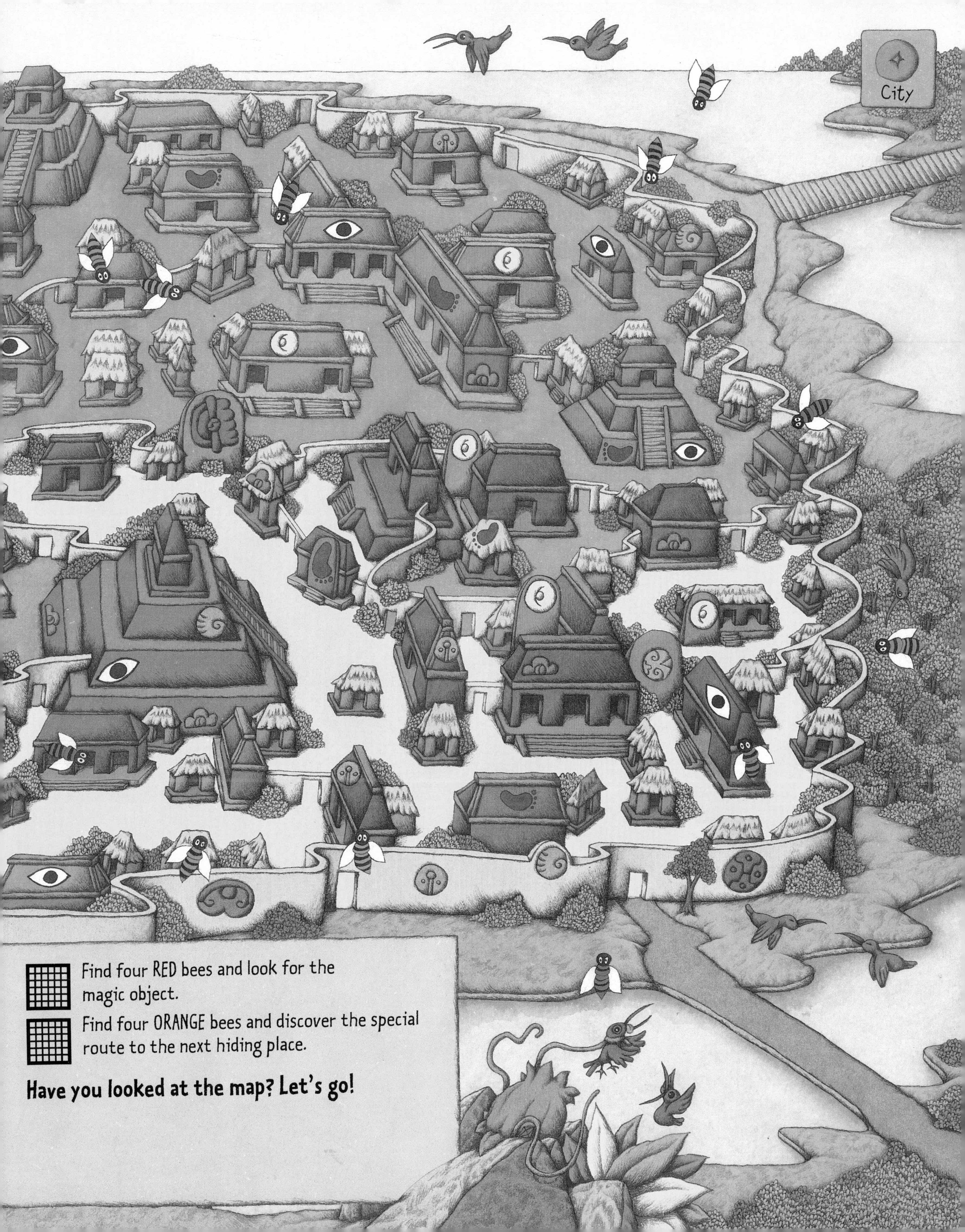
City

Find four RED bees and look for the magic object.

Find four ORANGE bees and discover the special route to the next hiding place.

Have you looked at the map? Let's go!

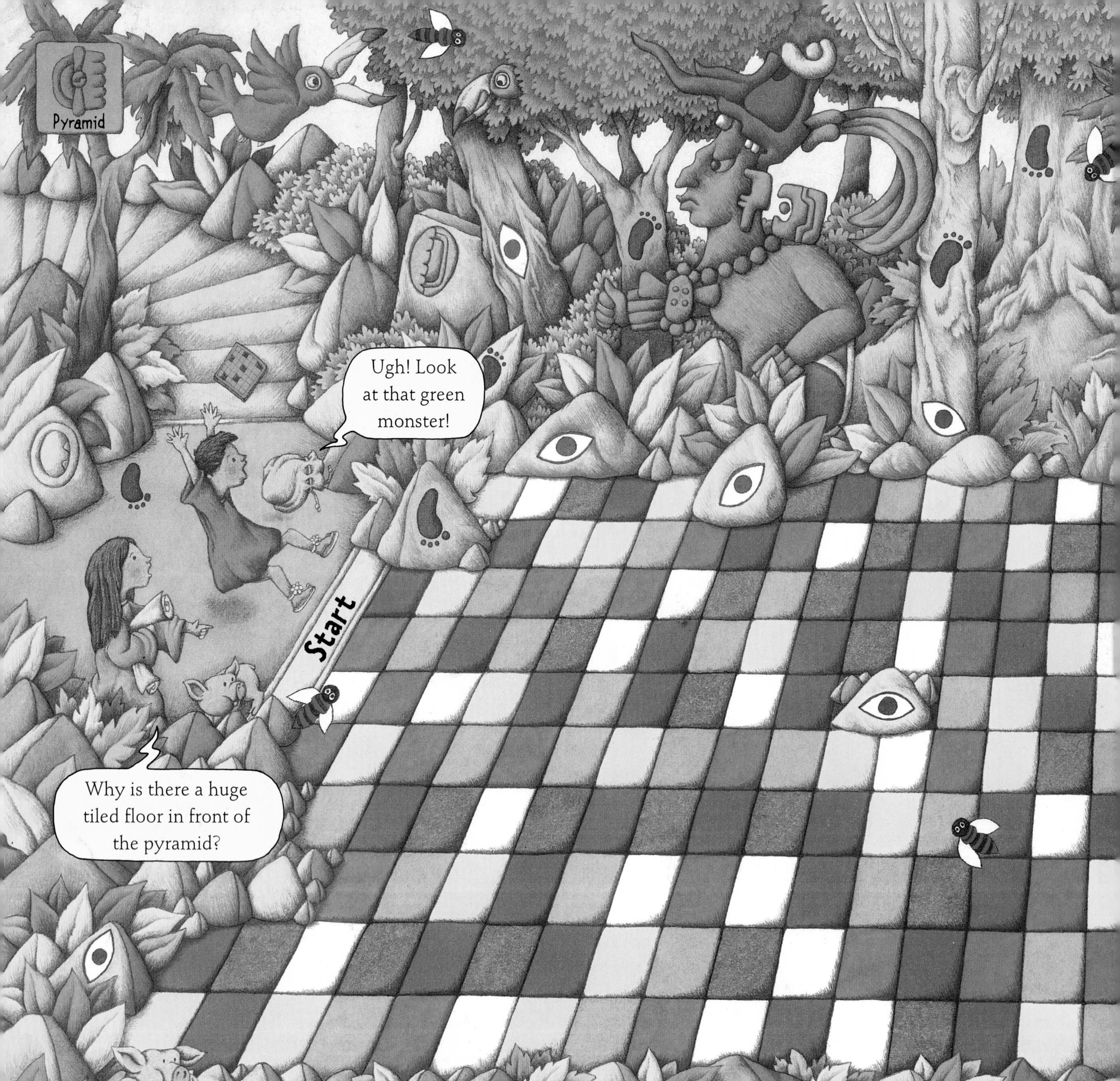
Pyramid
Ugh! Look at that green monster!
Start
Why is there a huge tiled floor in front of the pyramid?

The green monster is defending the pyramid. We have to cross the floor on colored tiles arranged in a particular order. The monster will attack if we get it wrong. Be warned—this is one of the hardest challenges we face.

Find four PURPLE bees. Then look for six different colors numbered 1 to 6. This is the color order. Leave the jade stone in this position on the picture to remind you of the order.

Starting with color number 1, use the color order to cross the floor from "Start" to "Finish" on tiles that touch. Do not move diagonally. Do not step on any tile more than once.

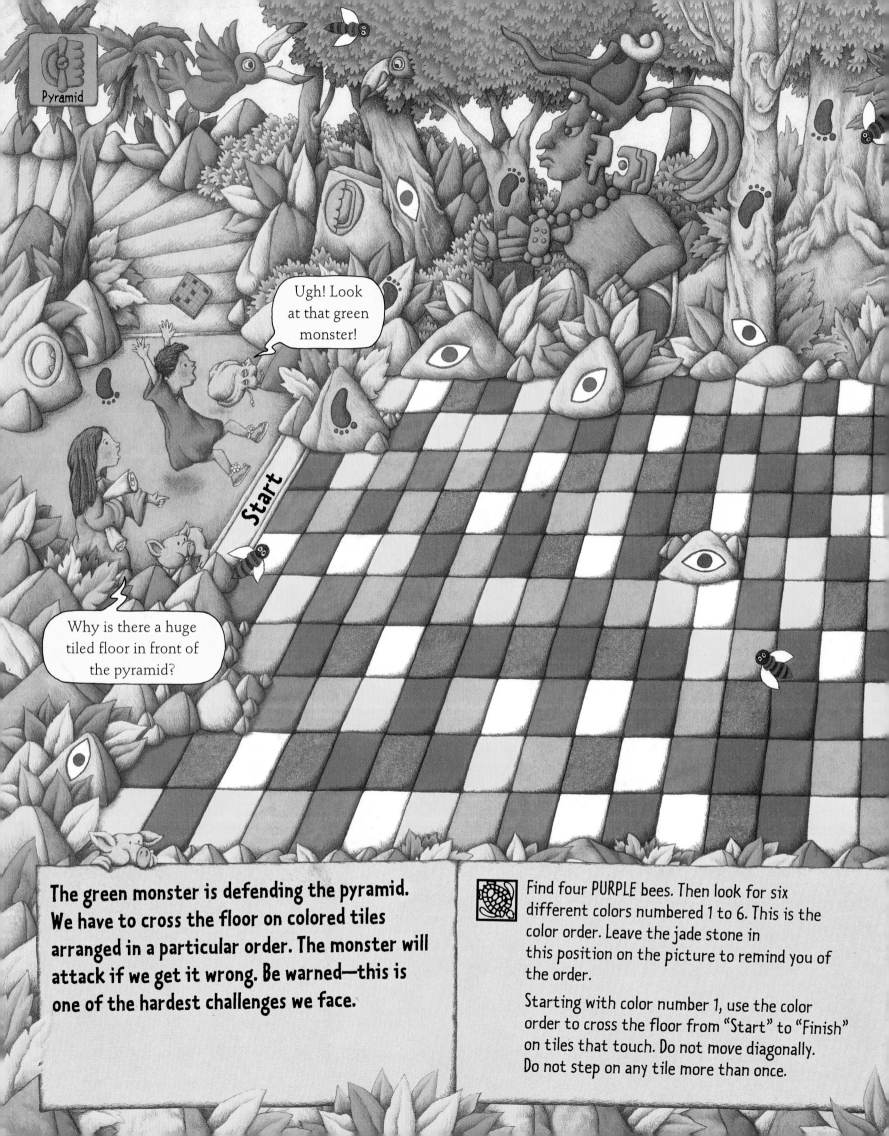

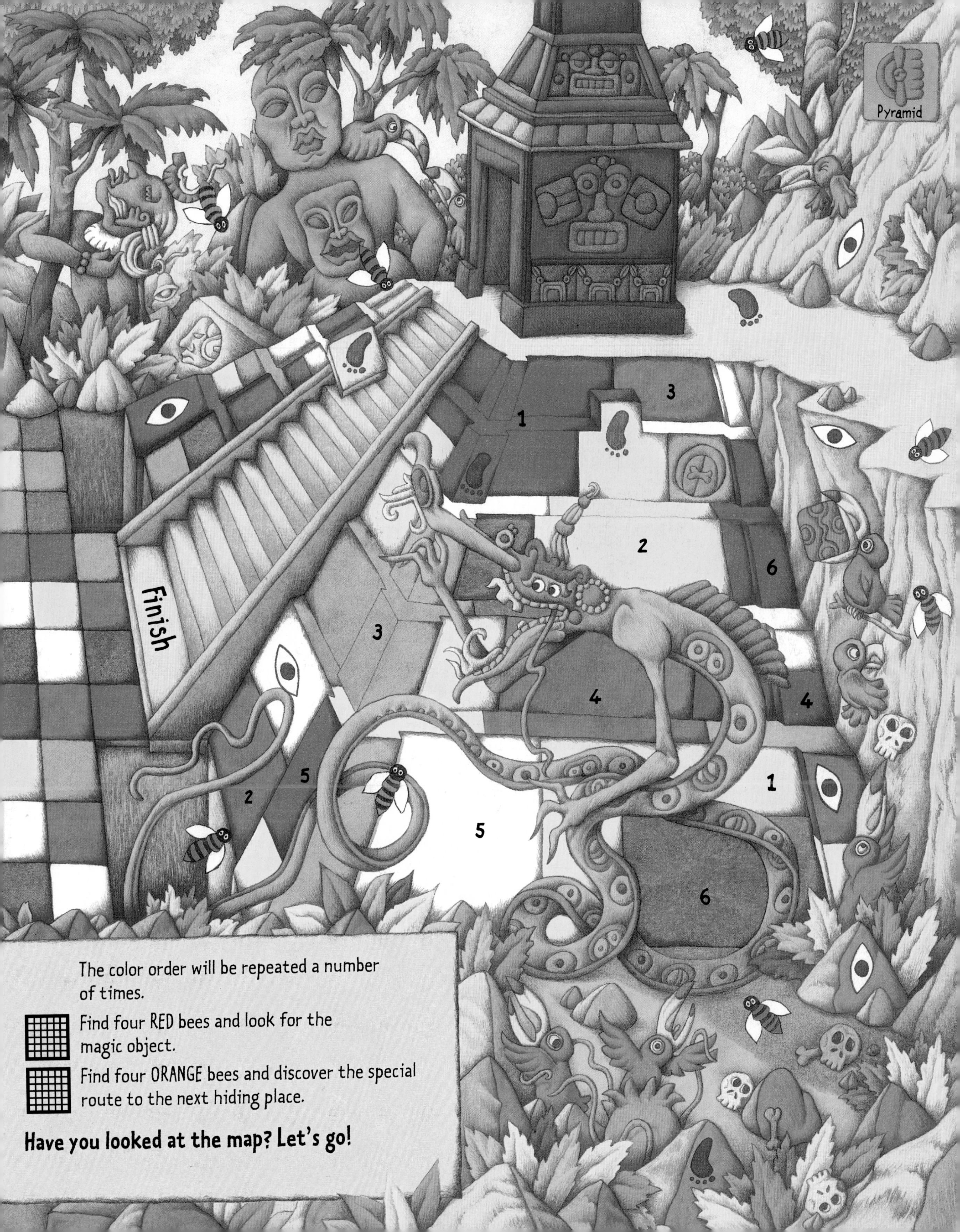

Pyramid
Finish
1
3
2
6
3
4
4
1
5
2
5
6

The color order will be repeated a number of times.

Find four RED bees and look for the magic object.

Find four ORANGE bees and discover the special route to the next hiding place.

Have you looked at the map? Let's go!

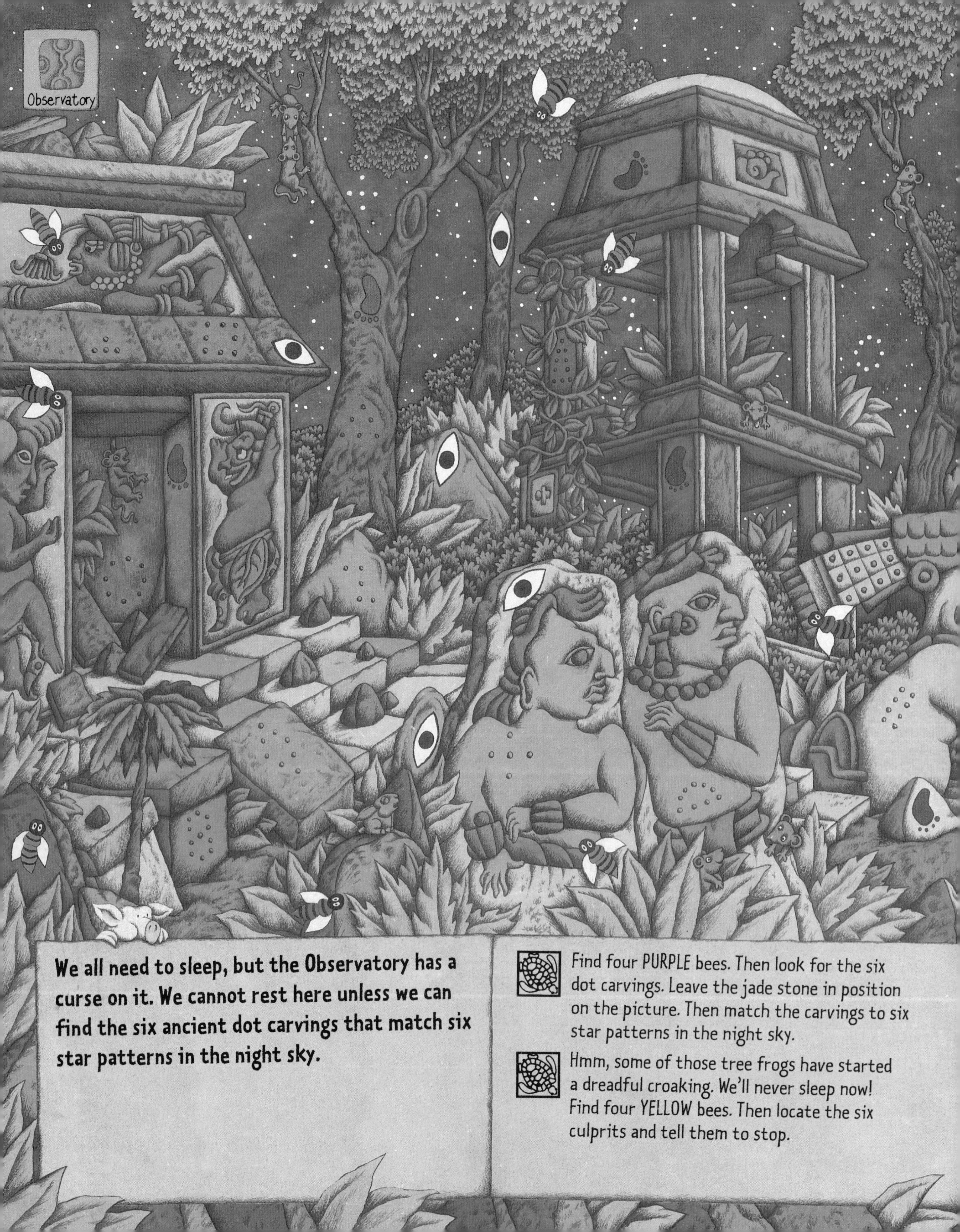
Observatory

We all need to sleep, but the Observatory has a curse on it. We cannot rest here unless we can find the six ancient dot carvings that match six star patterns in the night sky.

Find four PURPLE bees. Then look for the six dot carvings. Leave the jade stone in position on the picture. Then match the carvings to six star patterns in the night sky.

Hmm, some of those tree frogs have started a dreadful croaking. We'll never sleep now! Find four YELLOW bees. Then locate the six culprits and tell them to stop.

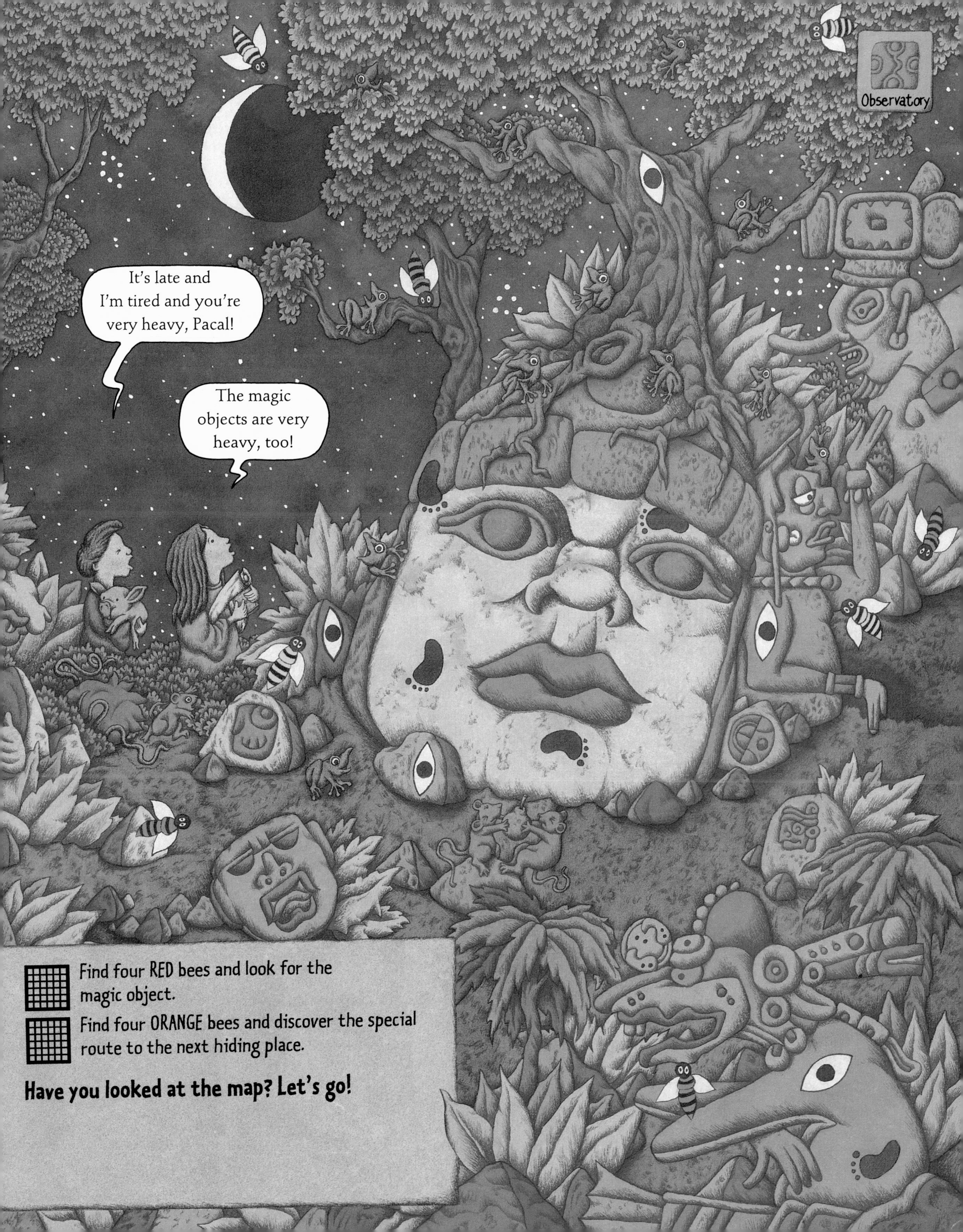
Observatory
It's late and I'm tired and you're very heavy, Pacal!
The magic objects are very heavy, too!

Find four RED bees and look for the magic object.

Find four ORANGE bees and discover the special route to the next hiding place.

Have you looked at the map? Let's go!

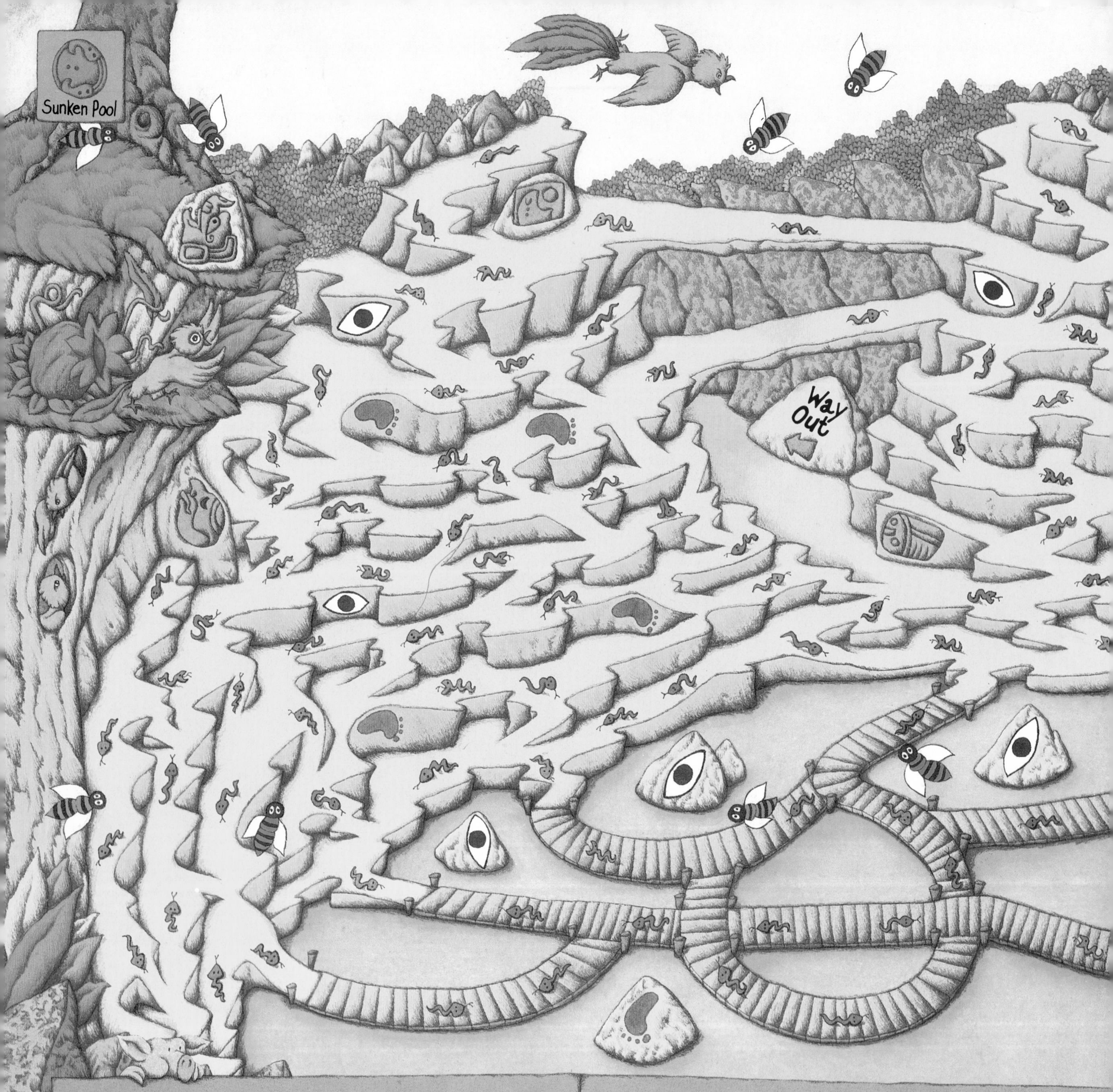
Sunken Pool
Way Out

There is only one safe route through the Sunken Pool maze and we must find it. Not all the snakes are dangerous—only ones of a particular color.

Find four PURPLE bees. When you can see six snakes that are all the same color, you have discovered the color of the dangerous ones.

Start where we are standing and make your way to the "Way Out" sign. Do not walk along any paths blocked by dangerous snakes.

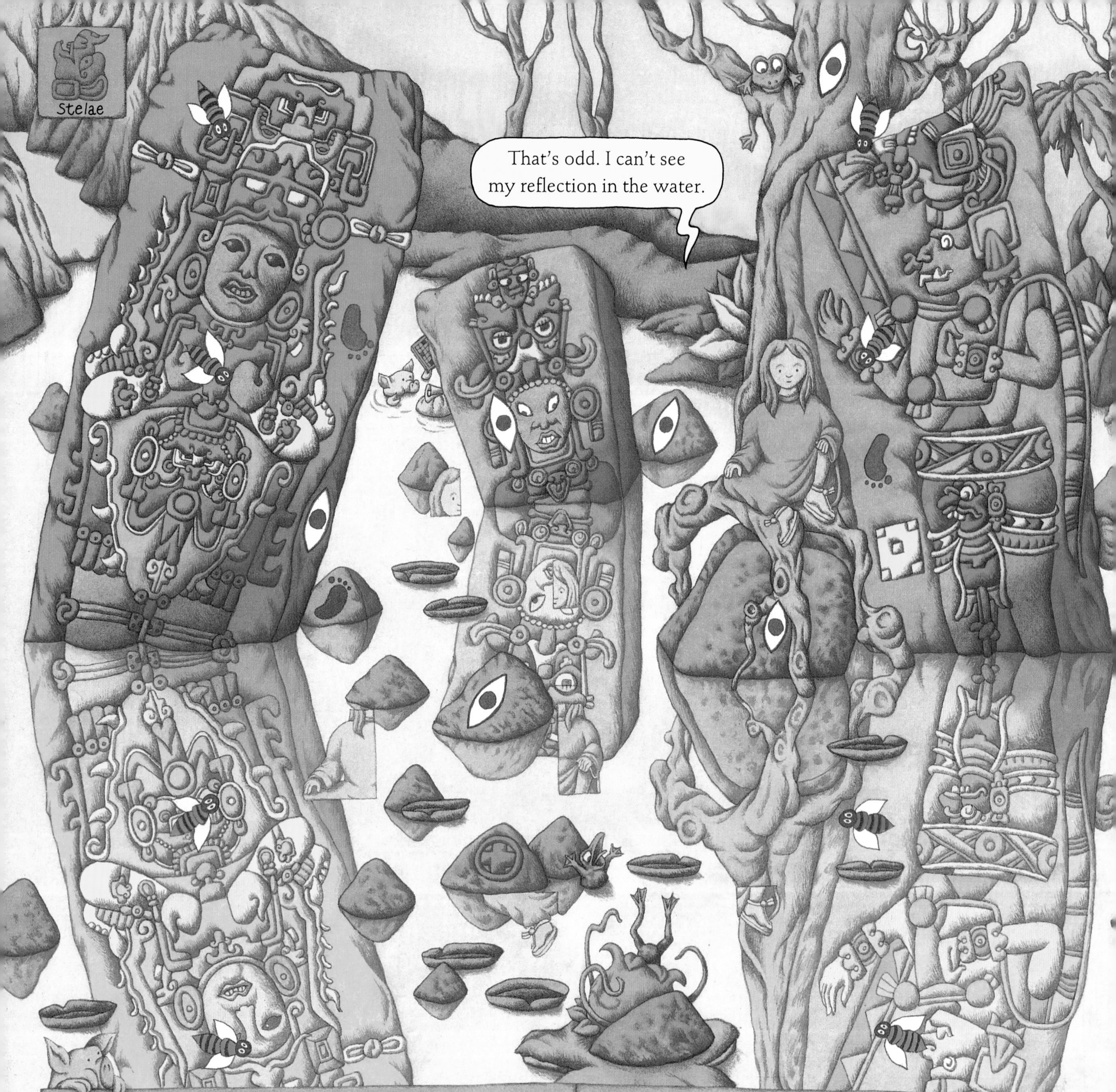
Stelae
That's odd. I can't see my reflection in the water.

Wicked alligator spirits have broken up Popol's and Xoc's reflections and have hidden the pieces. We may not continue until they have all been found.

Find four PURPLE bees near Xoc and look for the six pieces of her reflection. Then find another set of PURPLE bees near Popol and look for his reflection.

Six alligator spirits have disguised themselves and are lying in wait to bite your feet. YELLOW bees will help you find them.

Find four RED bees and look for the magic object.

Find four ORANGE bees and discover the special route to the next hiding place.

Have you looked at the map? Let's go!

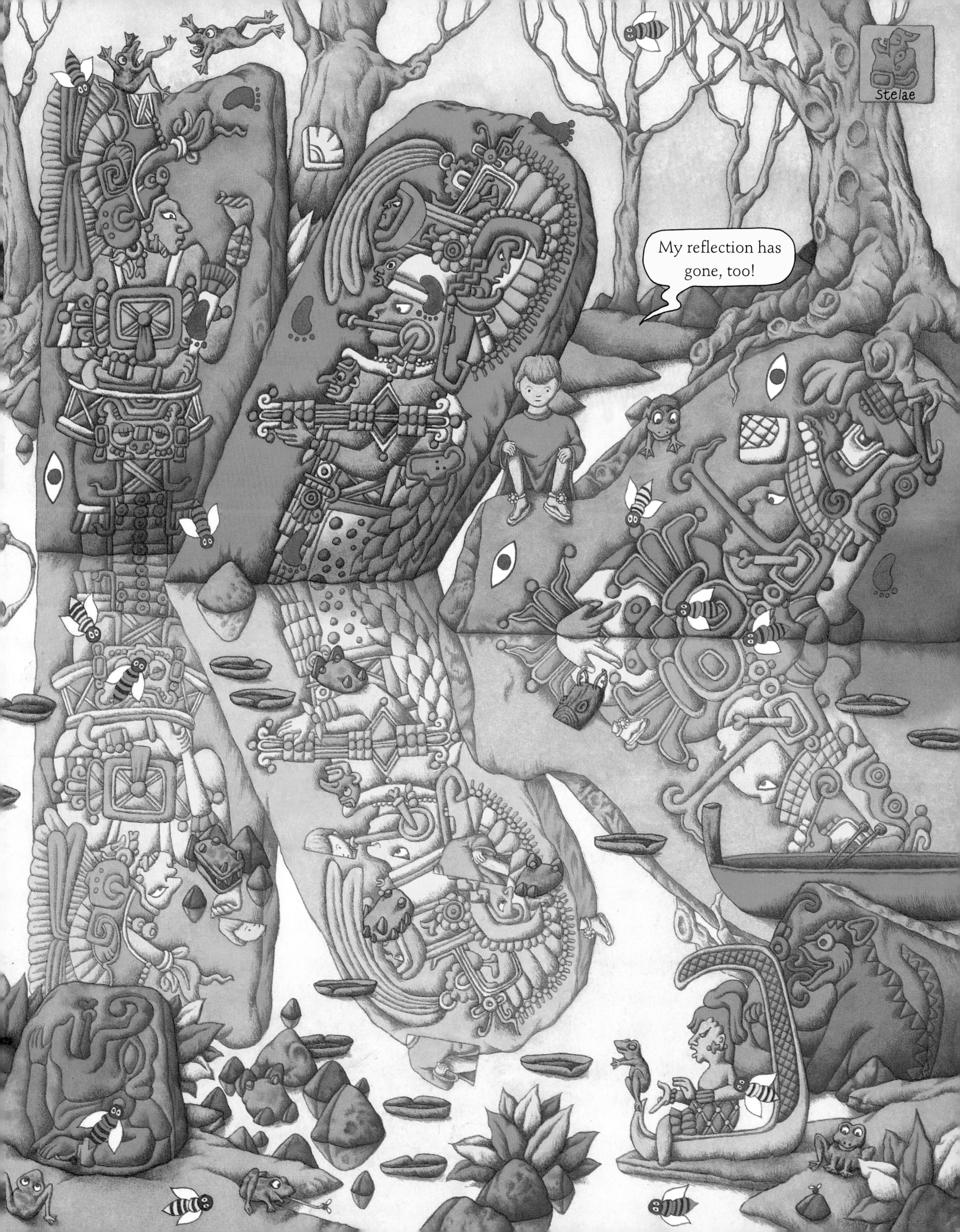
stelae
My reflection has gone, too!

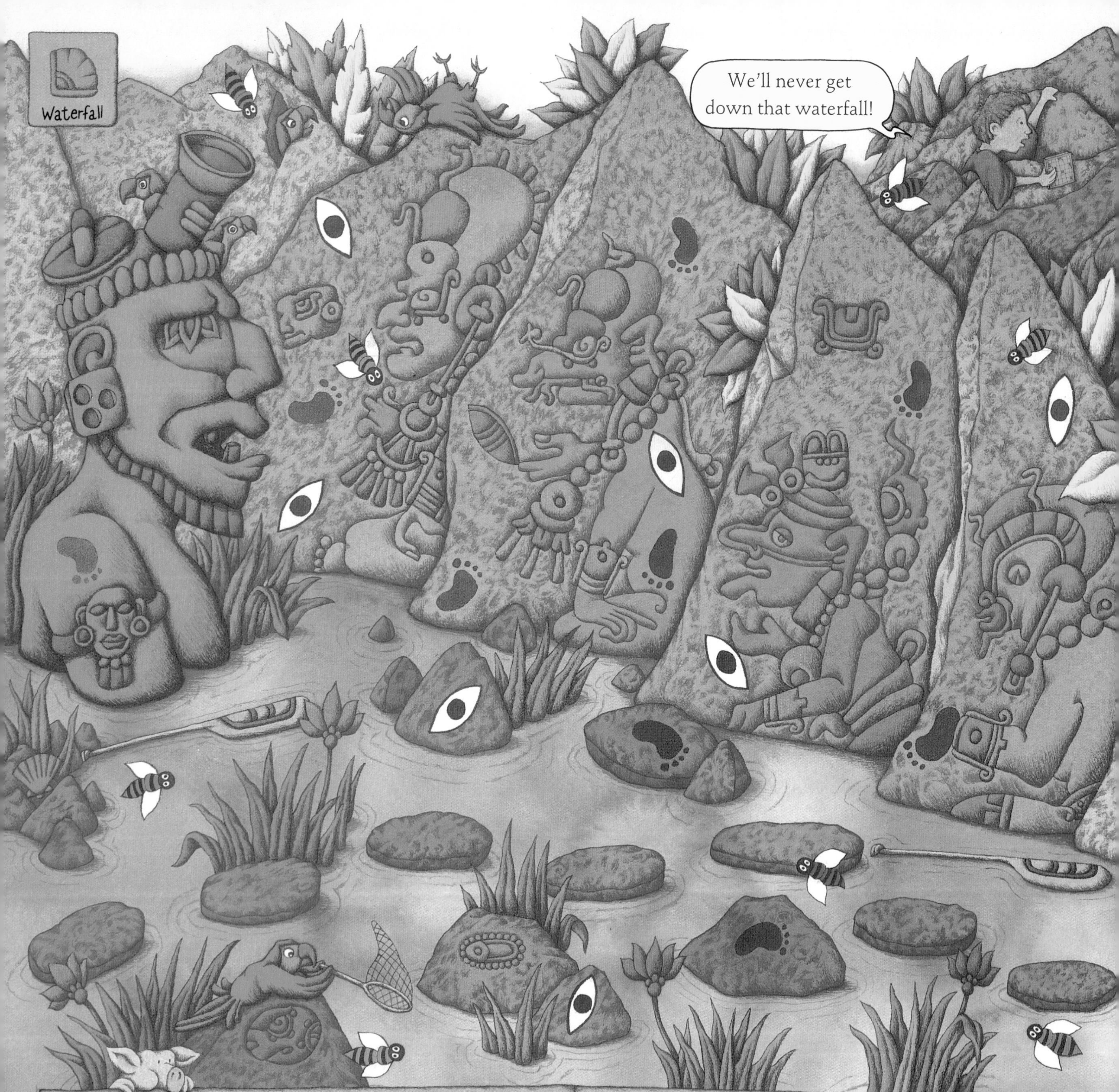
Waterfall
We'll never get down that waterfall!

Beware! This is a trap! Some of the rocks are slippery and if we step on them we will fall. There is one safe route down the waterfall. Listen carefully!

The slippery rocks are all the same color. Find four PURPLE bees. When you can see six rocks of the same color, you have found the color of the slippery rocks.

Start at the top of the waterfall on any rock that is not slippery. To reach the rock labeled "Finish" follow the direction of the arrows. If you land on a slippery rock, go back to the top and start again on a different rock.

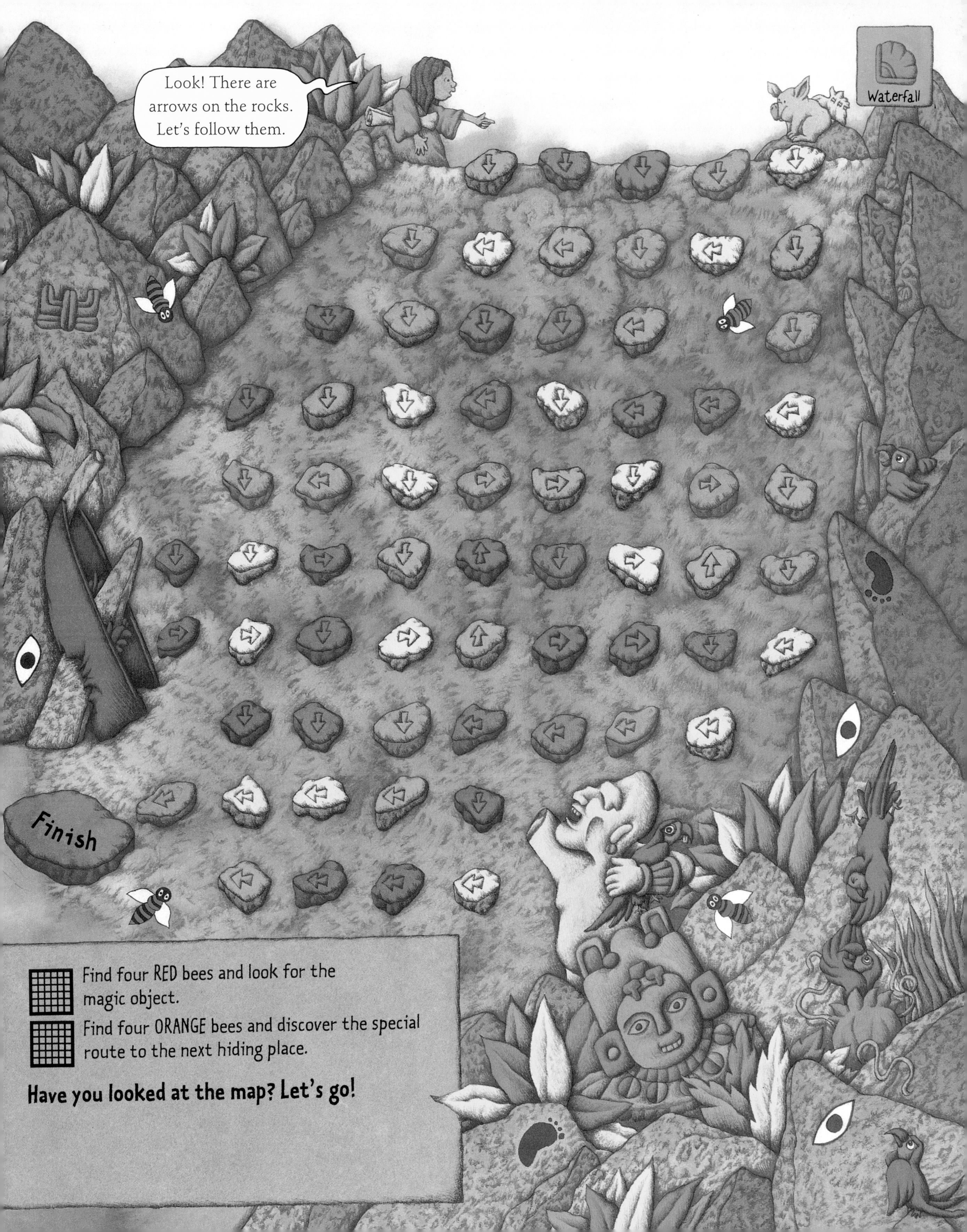
Look! There are arrows on the rocks. Let's follow them.
Waterfall
Finish

Find four RED bees and look for the magic object.

Find four ORANGE bees and discover the special route to the next hiding place.

Have you looked at the map? Let's go!

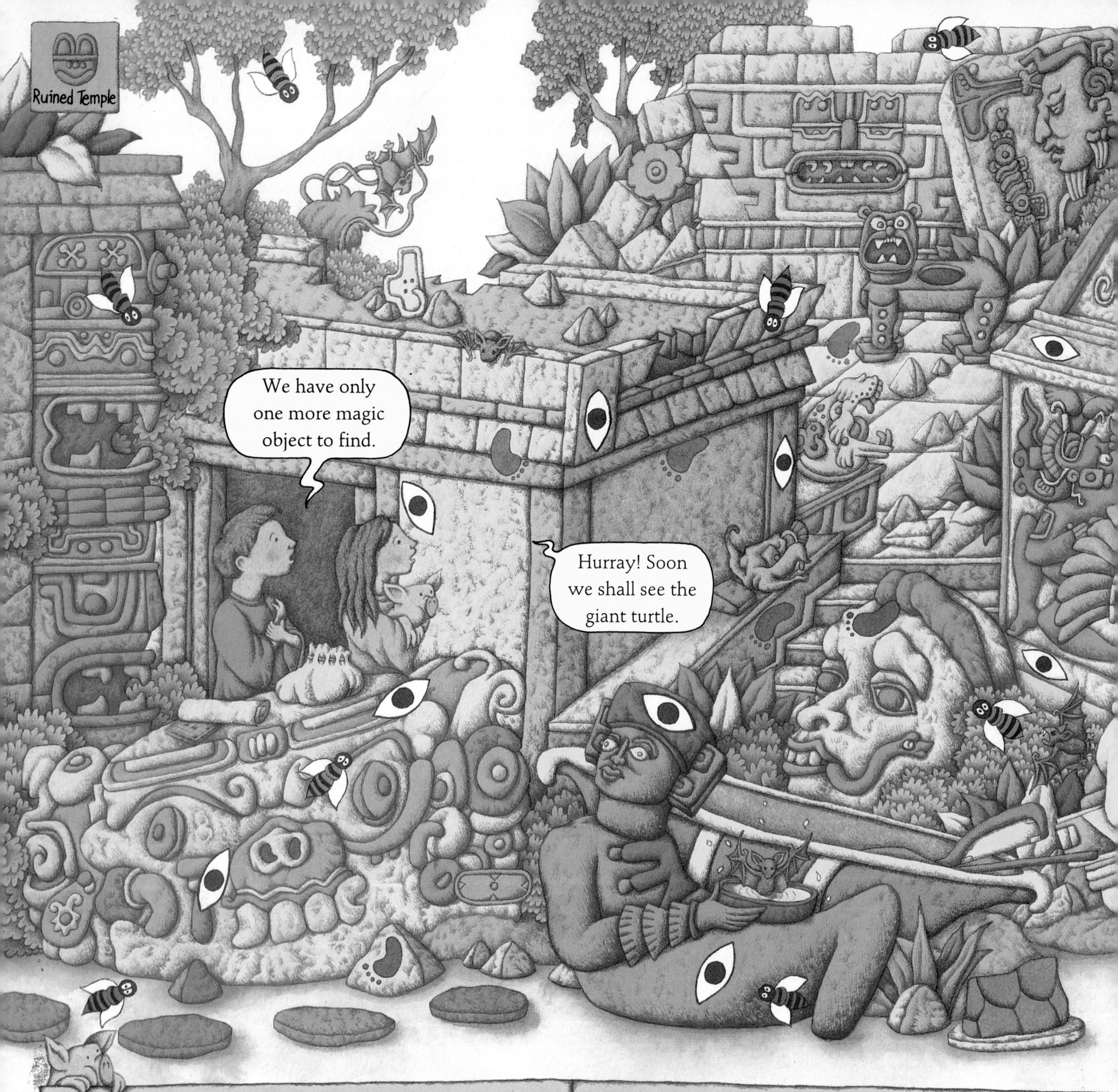

Ruined Temple
We have only one more magic object to find.
Hurray! Soon we shall see the giant turtle.

We ARE getting close to the giant turtle, but first we must overcome the greatest obstacle of all. Spirits have drained the power of the jade stone. To restore its power we must find the pieces of jade that complete its turtle image. But be warned—there are no purple bees to help us this time!

Move the jade stone around the picture until you can see pieces of jade through the six windows that complete its turtle image.

Find four RED bees and look for the magic object.

Find four ORANGE bees and discover the special route to the final hiding place.

Have you looked at the map? Let's go!

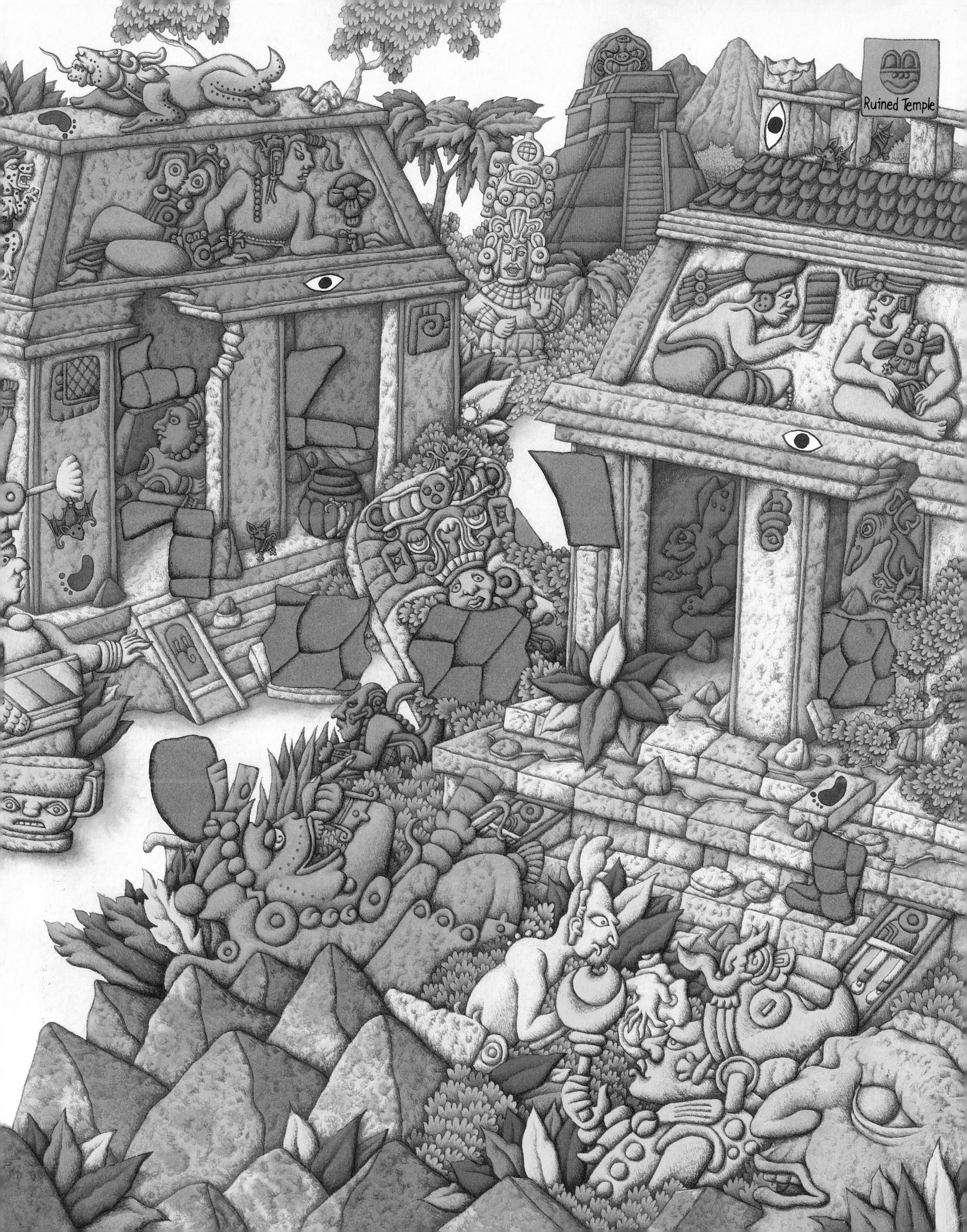
Ruined Temple

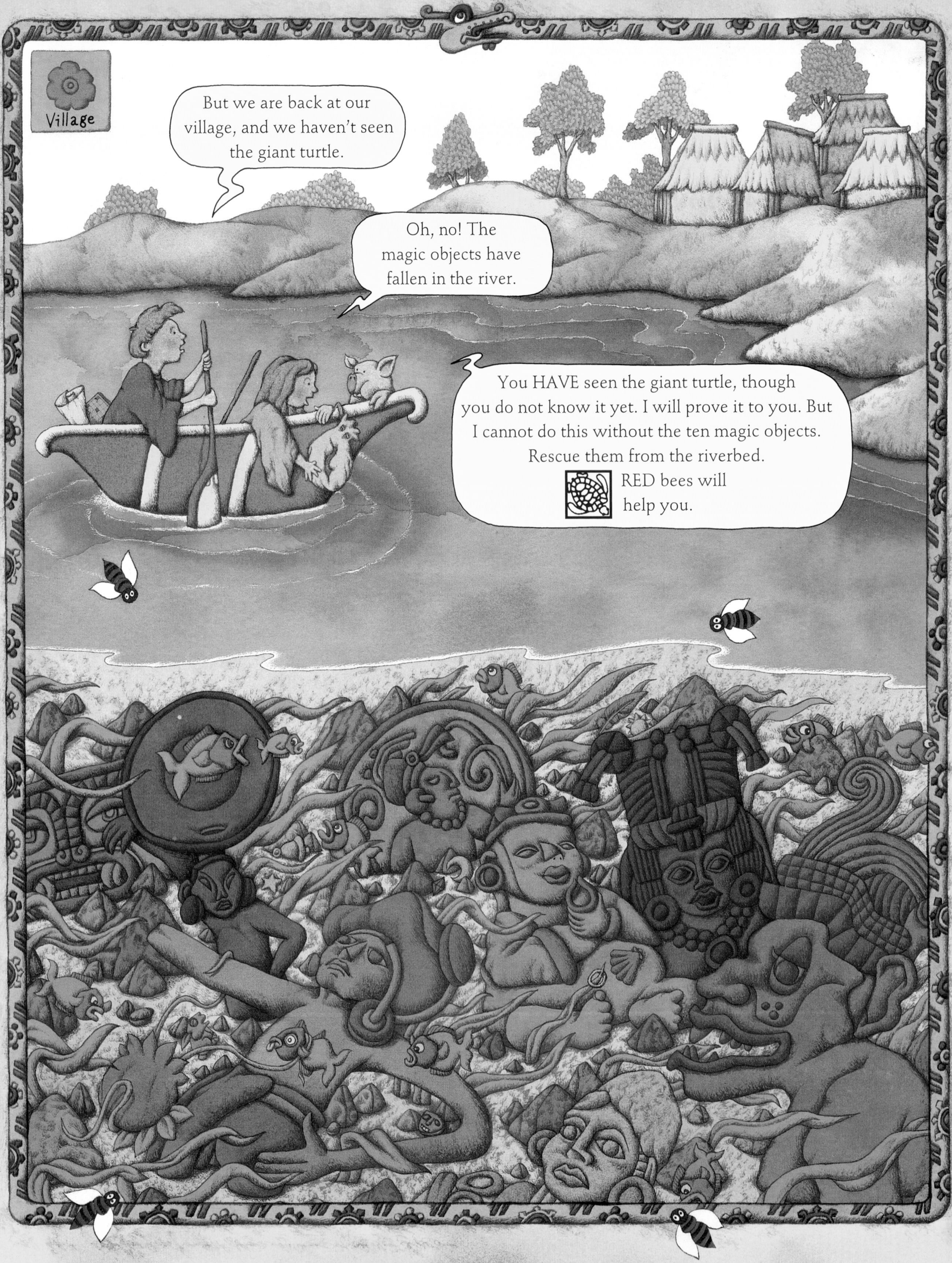
Village
But we are back at our village, and we haven't seen the giant turtle.
Oh, no! The magic objects have fallen in the river.
You HAVE seen the giant turtle, though you do not know it yet. I will prove it to you. But I cannot do this without the ten magic objects. Rescue them from the riverbed.
RED bees will help you.

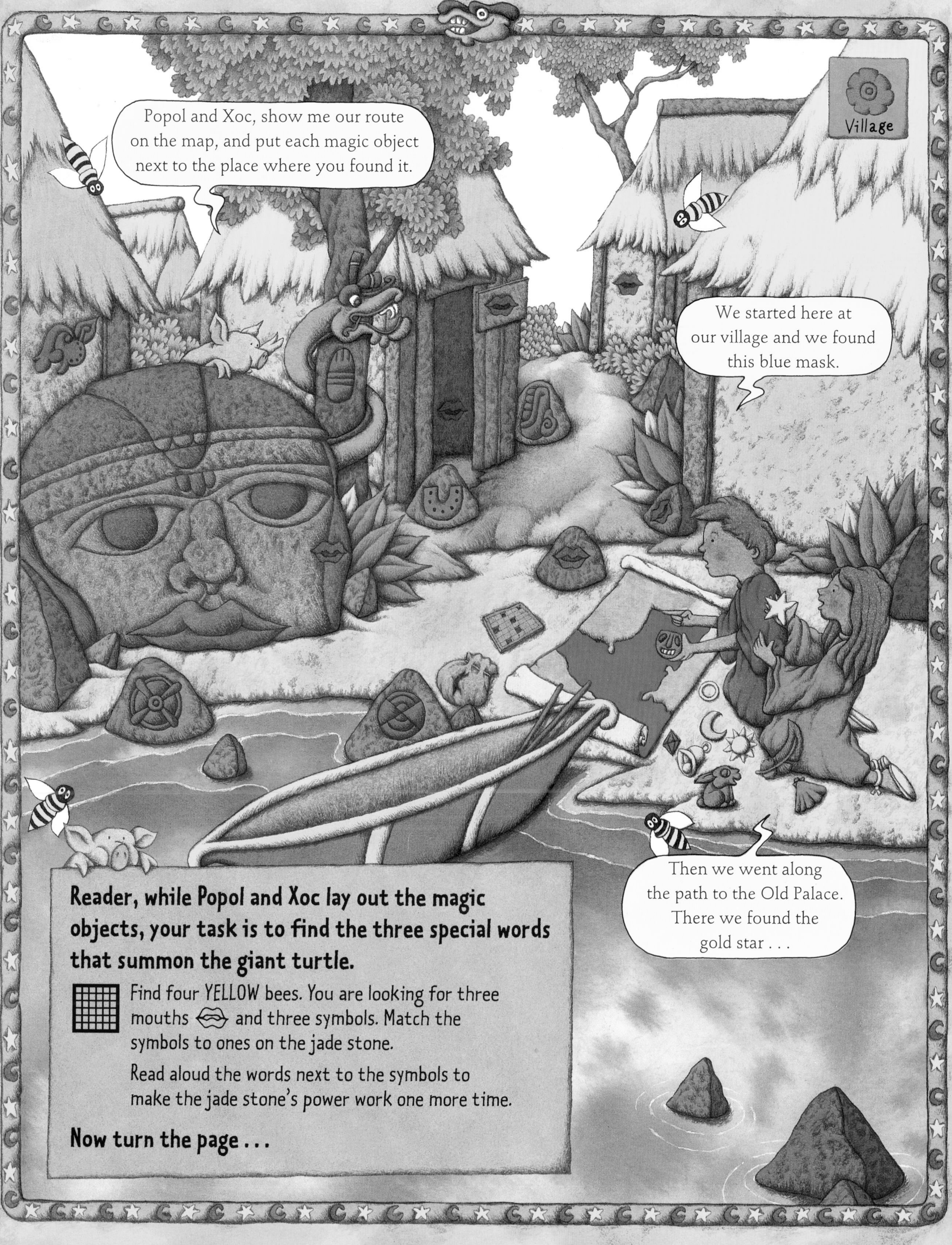
Village
Popol and Xoc, show me our route on the map, and put each magic object next to the place where you found it.
We started here at our village and we found this blue mask.
Then we went along the path to the Old Palace. There we found the gold star . . .

Reader, while Popol and Xoc lay out the magic objects, your task is to find the three special words that summon the giant turtle.

Find four *YELLOW* bees. You are looking for three mouths and three symbols. Match the symbols to ones on the jade stone.

Read aloud the words next to the symbols to make the jade stone's power work one more time.

Now turn the page . . .

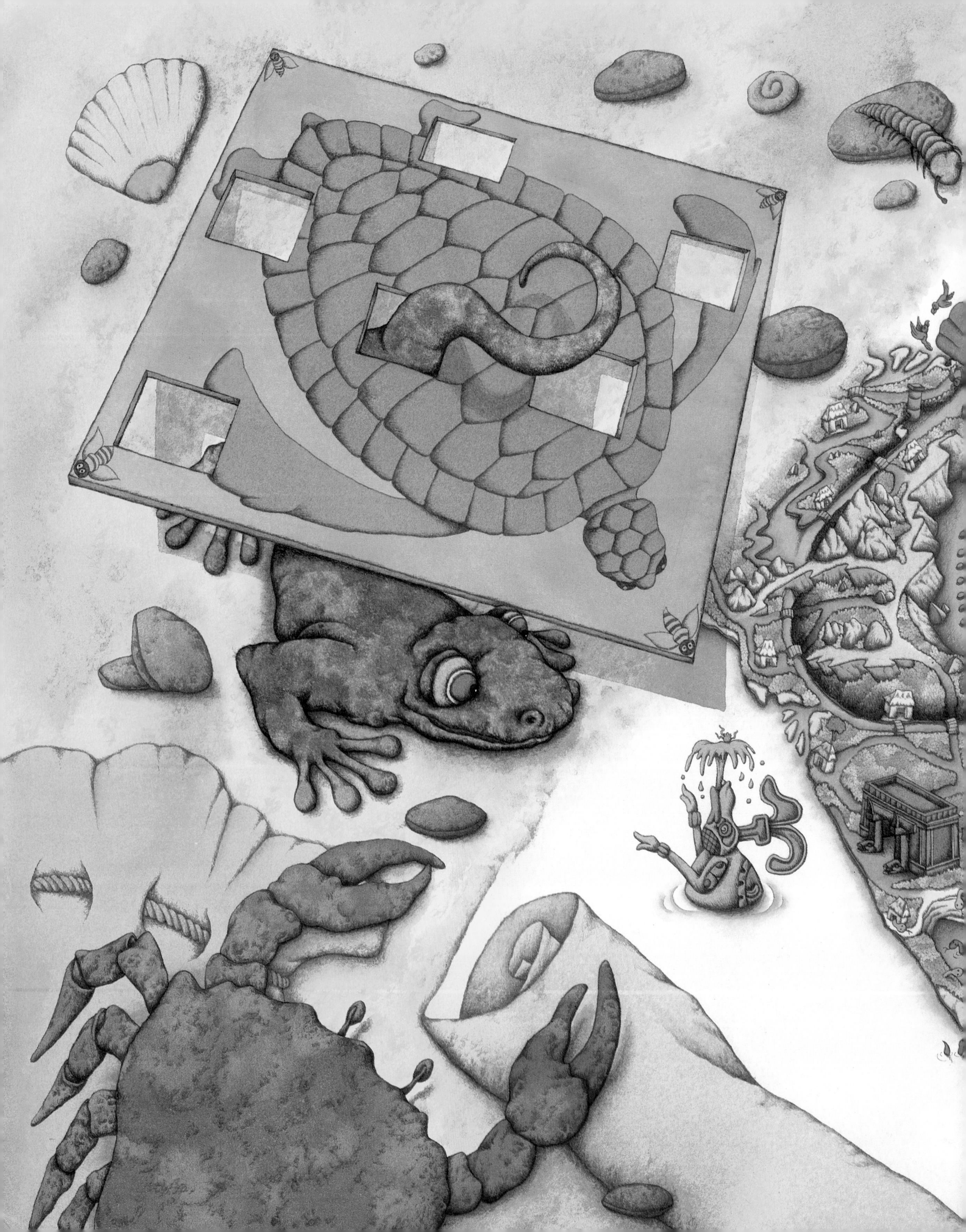

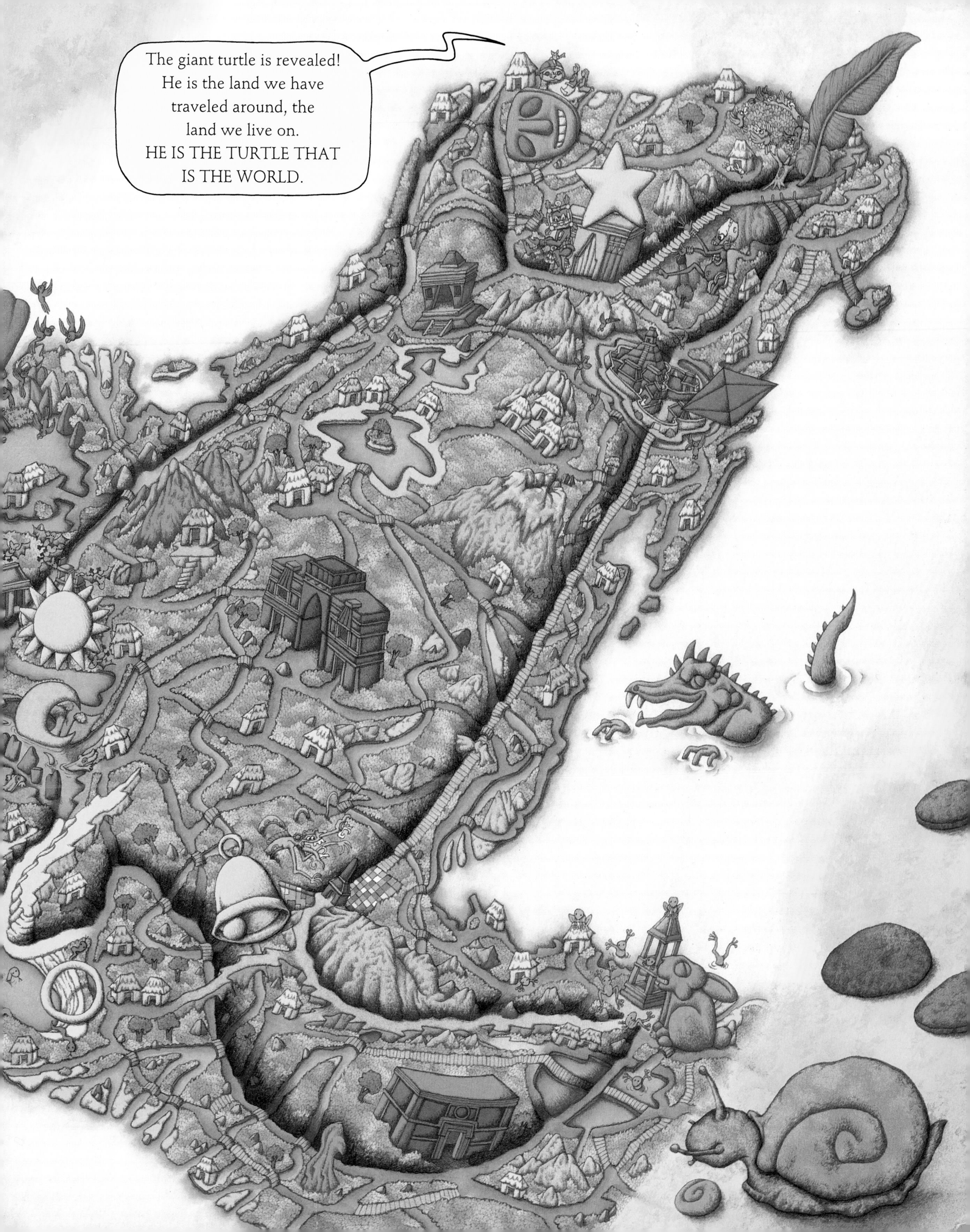
The giant turtle is revealed! He is the land we have traveled around, the land we live on. HE IS THE TURTLE THAT IS THE WORLD.

Popol and Xoc's village is in the north-west corner of the Yucatán in Mexico.

The Mayans lived in parts of Mexico and Central America.

Their great civilization was at its peak between A.D. 250 and 900. Later, they abandoned many of their cities.

POPOL AND XOC'S VILLAGE

Pacal is a peccary. PECCARIES are also called javelins because of their spearlike upper canines. When disturbed, they make a loud sound by rattling their teeth.

The Mayan world was divided into kingdoms. The kings ruled from their palaces in the cities.

Kings linked the people to the gods.

They sacrificed some of their own blood to honor the gods. This was taken from their veins by bloodletting.

OLD PALACE

ARMADILLOS have bands of armor to protect them. They swim well and swallow air to make themselves float. There are ten armadillos in the palace. Can you find them?

Trees were vital to the Mayans, as well as being sacred.

Trees provided medicine, fuel, building materials, and fruit.

Books were made out of bark paper. The Mayans could write anything with their sophisticated hieroglyphic writing.

RAVINE

RABBITS were linked to the moon goddess. The Mayans could see a rabbit on the moon's surface. There are ten rabbits near the ravine. Can you find them?

Mayan cities were centers of power. Their kings were often at war with other rulers.

In the center of the cities were beautifully decorated palaces, temples, pyramids, and houses for the nobles.

Most people lived in the surrounding countryside.

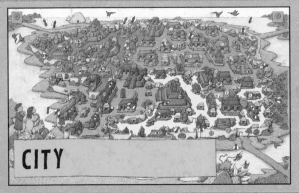

CITY

The Mayans linked HUMMING-BIRDS to bloodletting because of the way they drink nectar from flowers. There are ten hummingbirds near the city. Can you find them?

Many stepped pyramids were built over the tombs of kings and nobles.

Ancestor worship was important to the Mayans. Pyramids provided a center for this.

Pyramids were also believed to be sacred mountains—the temples on the top were close to the gods in the sky.

PYRAMID

A TOUCAN's bill is often a third of the bird's length. It juggles fruit in its bill and tosses back its head to swallow. There are ten toucans near the pyramid. Can you find them?